It was a beautiful day and
George was curious.
He was curious about all the
boats on the river.

George liked one boat best of all.
It was carrying cars!
"That is a ferryboat," said the man
with the yellow hat.

George liked to boat watch but
he was eager to get to the lake.
If he was lucky, he might see
another ferryboat.

At the lake
there were lots of people.
They were watching the model
boat contest.
There were boats of all kinds.

Bill showed George his model
sailboat.
George thought it was wonderful.

"I saved a lot of
money to build this boat," Bill said.
"Will you keep it safe until the
contest?"

George was happy to help.
He held the boat very carefully.

He looked at the boat.
He looked at his toy cars.
George had an idea.

George made Bill's boat look just like a ferryboat.

Oh, no!
It sank.
What would Bill enter into the
contest now?

George tried to make another
boat for Bill out of his toys.
It sank, too.
George saw that some of the toys
floated.
He had a better idea.

George looked at other boats
on the river.
He made plans to build a boat
from his floating toys.
Bill would be proud.

When Bill came back, he saw the
new boat.
"That is a great ferryboat!" Bill said.

Then George showed Bill what
had happened to the sailboat.

"Uh-oh!" Bill said.
"I forgot to shut the boat's windows.
I'll fix that.

Now water cannot get inside and the boat will float.
Let's go enter our boats in the contest!"

Everyone won a blue ribbon for
all their hard work—even George.

Ships Ahoy!

Make a paper boat.

1. Take a sheet of paper and fold it in half.

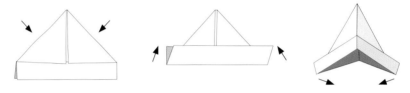

2. Fold down the top corners.   3. Fold up the bottom flaps.   4. Fold into the center.

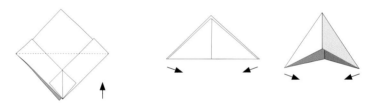

5. Fold up the bottom half of one side. Repeat on the other side.

6. Push sides in and pull center toward you.

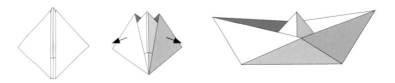

7. Pull sides away from each other to make your boat!

Now test your boat and see if it floats.

To the Top

Gather the household items listed below. Ask a grownup to fill up the bathroom tub or sink, and see if they float!

 Float

 Sink

 Did you guess correctly?

Margarine tub

Pencil

Egg carton

Magnet

Flower

Wooden block

Crayon

Rubber ball

Plastic spoon

Metal spoon

Challenge: Watermelon

For information about permission to reproduce selections from this book, write to
Permissions, Houghton Mifflin Company, 215 Park Avenue South, New York, New York 10003.

Library of Congress Cataloging-in-Publication Data is on file.

ISBN-13: 978-0-618-89196-2

Design by Afsoon Razavi

www.houghtonmifflinbooks.com

Manufactured in Singapore
TWP 10 9 8 7 6 5 4 3 2 1

The Boat Show

Adaptation by Kate O'Sullivan
Based on the TV series teleplay
written by Raye Lankford

Houghton Mifflin Company
Boston 2008